D0574297

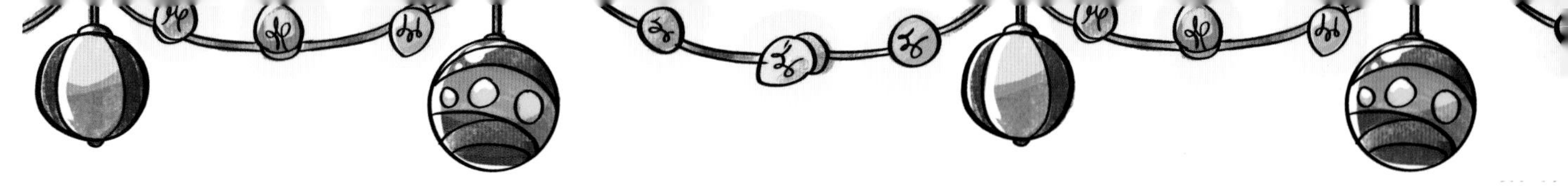

For all the moms, who deserve our appreciation for keeping the family sleigh running smoothly. And for our moms, Jody, Karen, and Meg, who did this for us and much more.

www.mascotbooks.com

Claudia Claus & the Christmas Eve Storm

©2017 Ann and Rob Quandt. All Rights Reserved. No part of this publication may be reproduced, stored in a retrieval system or transmitted in any form by any means electronic, mechanical, or photocopying, recording or otherwise without the permission of the author.

For more information, please contact:
Mascot Books
620 Herndon Parkway, Suite 320
Herndon, VA 20170
info@mascotbooks.com

Library of Congress Control Number: 2017911375

CPSIA Code: PRT1017A
ISBN-13: 978-1-63177-918-3

Printed in the United States

Claudia Claus
& the Christmas Eve Storm
Written by Ann & Rob Quandt
Illustrated by Yoko Matsuoka

It is two days before *Christmas*, and **Claudia Claus** is busy making sure everything is checked twice.

Santa may deliver the presents but keeping up with the letters, managing the elves, and figuring out who has been naughty or nice is up to **Claudia**.

Charlie B

Claudia scooters into the mailroom where the elves are opening all the letters from children around the world. The elves are having trouble finding the correct address for Charlie B. who has been a very good boy this year.

"Hi, **Mrs. Claus**. Charlie B. wrote us a letter from Chicago asking for a bike for Christmas, but we aren't seeing that address in the E.L.F. system."

"Remember that sometimes kids move. It looks like Charlie B. may have moved to San Francisco this year. Moving is tough for kids, so it will be wonderful to cheer him up with a new bike!"

Next, Claudia stops by the Toy Department to see how toy production is coming. With only two more days until Christmas Eve, the elves are busy.

"Hi, Claudia. We finished making the teddy bears and baseball bats and are just finalizing the scooter production. Scooters are the most popular toy this year!"

"That's great!" says Claudia. "I love my scooter, so I'm sure all of the kids will too."

EXIT

Claudia scooters over to the Transportation Depot. The elves are busy tuning up Santa's sleigh while Santa feeds the reindeer.

"Hi, Claudia. The sleigh is as good as new! You can't even tell where Santa backed into that chimney last year. We'll start loading it up tonight."

"I heard that!" Santa yells. "It wasn't my fault. That was a tight space, and I couldn't see over the stack of presents!"

Claudia laughs. “I know, dear. We added a back-up camera to the sleigh to help you out. Speaking of taking care of you, maybe you could have a few less cookies and a few more carrots this year?”

“I’ll try, but Emilie in Paris makes amazing macaroons, and Marcus in Toronto makes the best chocolate chip cookies in the world!”

Later that day, **Claudia** stops by the Control Center to check on Santa's flight path. "How does the weather look for Christmas Eve? Any storms we'll need to fly around?"

"There is a big storm above Greenland that we're closely watching. Santa will have to fly around it, but he should still have time to deliver all the presents."

On *Christmas Eve*, **Claudia** holds a team meeting. "Thanks for all of your hard work this holiday season. Any last minute updates? How about the mailroom team?"

"We moved two more children from the naughty list to the nice list. They apologized, and they meant it. Unfortunately, Donald in Washington, D.C., is still going to get a lump of coal—he hasn't been very nice this year."

Claudia nods and checks off her list. Next, it's the Toy Department's turn. "It was down to the wire, but all the scooters are packaged and ready to go."

Claudia writes a few more notes down, while the Transportation Depot gives their report. "The sleigh is loaded, and the Reindeer Radio is up and running so we can talk to Santa during his trip."

"Great job!" says Claudia. "Control Center?"

"The storm over Greenland is getting bigger. This might be the biggest *Christmas Eve* storm we've ever seen!"

"Got it," says Claudia. "We'll have to be careful with Santa's route."

After getting the go-ahead from all of the departments at the North Pole, Claudia clears Santa for takeoff.

"*Merry Christmas* to all!" Santa calls as he climbs into his sleigh. "We are going to make a lot of little girls and boys happy tonight."

Claudia and the North Pole team work through the night to help Santa stay on schedule, but the storm has picked up pace and is heading right for him.

"Oh no, we'll have to call Santa on the Reindeer Radio," says Claudia.

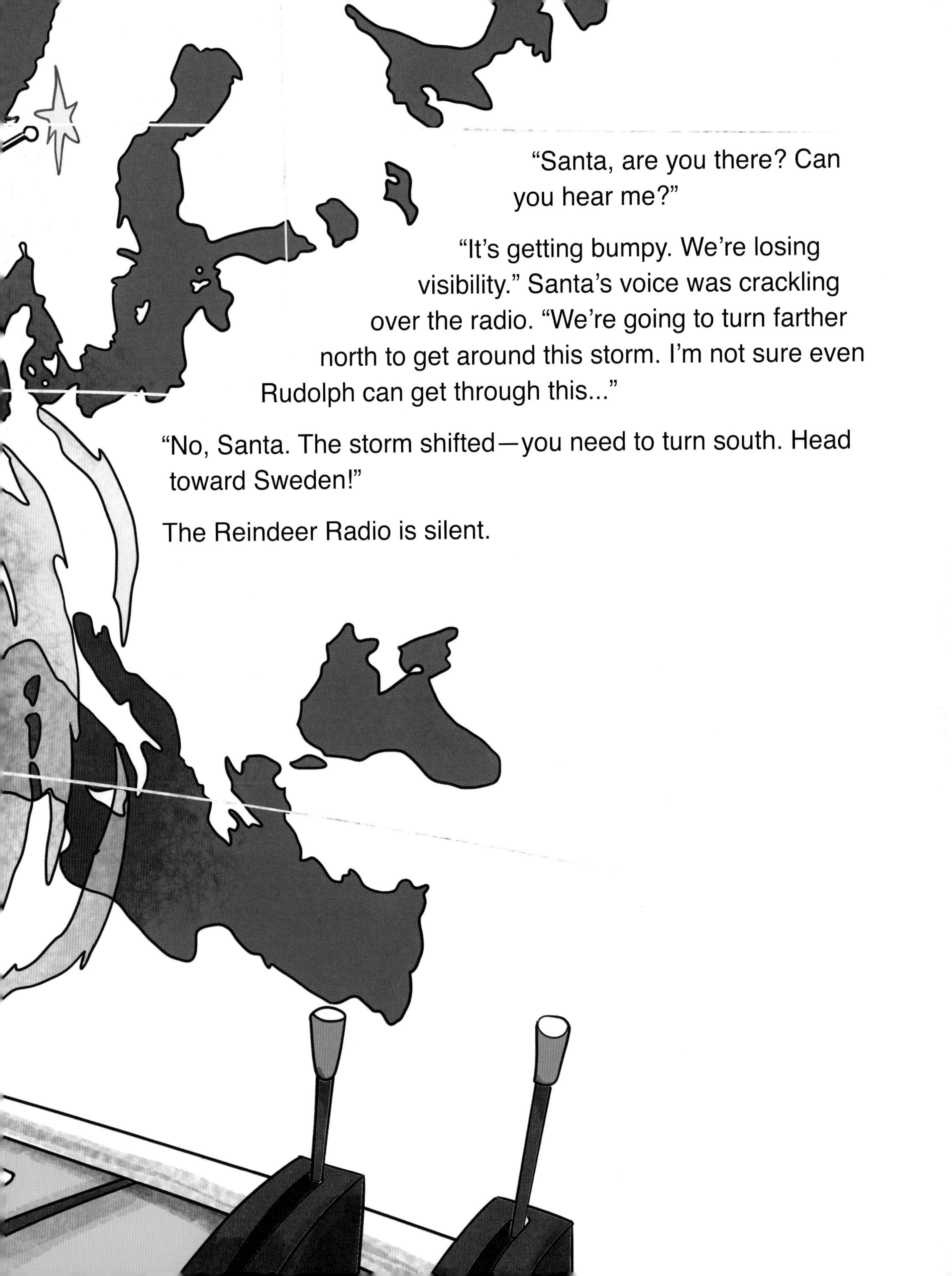

"Santa, are you there? Can you hear me?"

"It's getting bumpy. We're losing visibility." Santa's voice was crackling over the radio. "We're going to turn farther north to get around this storm. I'm not sure even Rudolph can get through this..."

"No, Santa. The storm shifted—you need to turn south. Head toward Sweden!"

The Reindeer Radio is silent.

Claudia and the elves anxiously wait in the control center.

Suddenly, they hear Santa's voice over the radio. "Ho, ho, ho! That was quite a bumpy ride, but we are safely on Annika's roof in Sweden."

“So glad you’re okay,
dear. Should be smooth
sleigh riding from here!”

With **Claudia's** help, the rest of Santa's trip is storm-free and present-full. He delivers all the presents with only seconds to spare.

Santa and the reindeer return to the North Pole exhausted from their world journey.

"*Merry Christmas*, Santa. Welcome home."

"*Merry Christmas*, Claudia. We couldn't have done it without you and the elves. I can't wait for next year!"

About Ann and Rob

Ann found it challenging each year to hear her children idolize Santa Claus when there was no female equivalent. In response, Ann came up with the idea of a modern Mrs. Claus as the leader of the entire North Pole back-end operation—an equal to Santa in children's admiration.

When they are not writing children's stories (which is pretty much all the time as this is their first), Ann and Rob are busy working full-time in Boston and raising their three young children. While the Quandt house does not run nearly as smoothly as the North Pole does, in writing this book, Ann and Rob did want to impress upon their children how they run their family…as a team.